EVERYTHING IS
MAMA

To Winnie, Franny, and Nancy. You are my everything.

A FEIWEL AND FRIENDS BOOK
An imprint of Macmillan Publishing Group, LLC
175 Fifth Avenue, New York, NY 10010

Our books may be purchased for promotional, educational, or business use. Please contact your
local bookseller or the Macmillan Corporate and Premium Sales Department at (800) 221-7945
ext. 5442 or by e-mail at MacmillanSpecialMarkets@macmillan.com.

Library of Congress Control Number: 2017940441

ISBN 978-1-250-12584-2

Book design by Rich Deas and Miguel Ordóñez

Feiwel and Friends logo designed by Filomena Tuosto

First edition, 2017

1   3   5   7   9   10   8   6   4   2

mackids.com

EVERYTHING IS
MAMA

JIMMY FALLON

ILLUSTRATED BY MIGUEL ORDÓÑEZ

FEIWEL AND FRIENDS
NEW YORK

Everything is Mama
according to you.

But there are **other** fun words
you'll want to know, too.

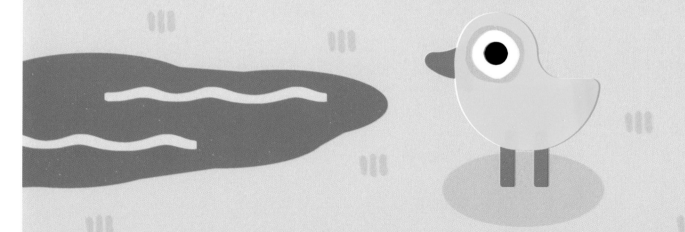

BALLOON

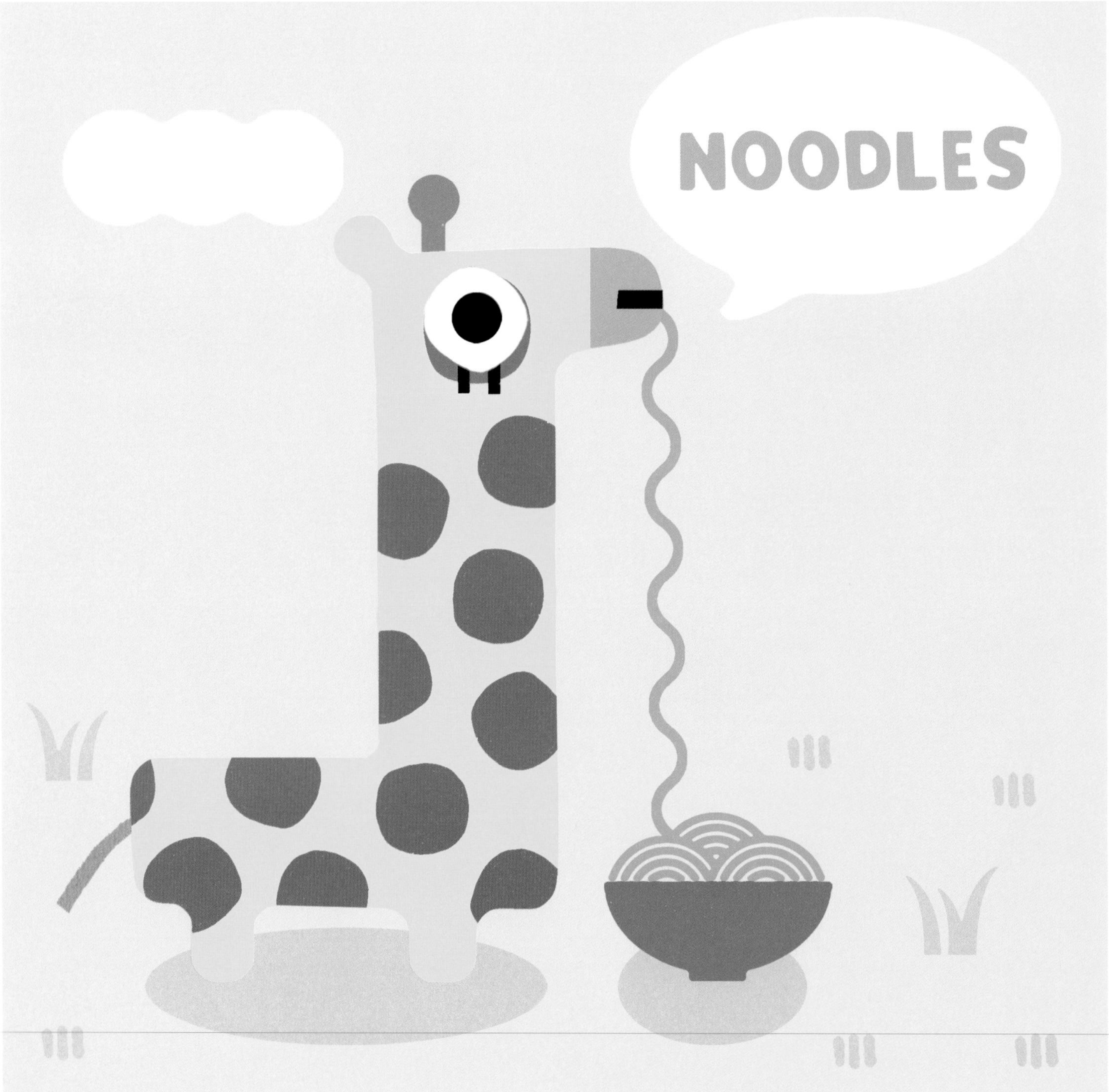
NOODLES

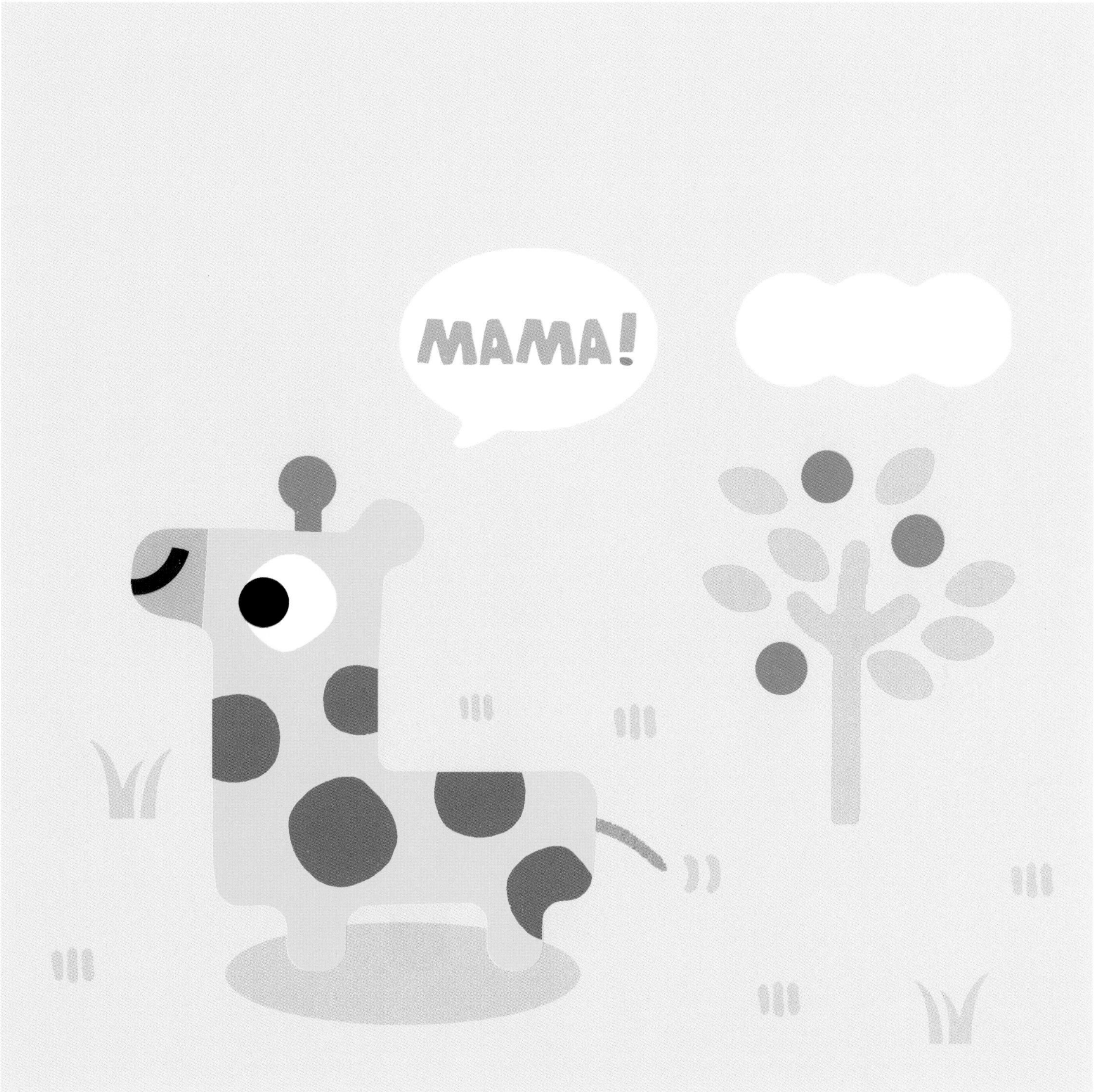
MAMA!

Everything is Mama
according to you.

But one day you'll see,
Mama's EVERYTHING is YOU.